Franklin Watts Australia
Level 17/207 Kent Street
Sydney, NSW 2000

A CIP catalogue record for this book
is available from the British Library.

ISBN: 978 0 7496 7715 2

Printed in Great Britain

Franklin Watts is a division of Hachette Children's Books,
an Hachette Livre UK company.

Snap Kick

Spike T. Adams

Illustrated by Jade

W

FRANKLIN WATTS
LONDON•SYDNEY

Chapter 1

I'm waiting my turn.

Gonna show Mr Sands what I can do.

Out there, on the pitch.

I'm a pretty good player.

Every year I try out for the team.

But every year I mess up.

Just gotta keep my cool.

And get past Mikey Stone and his crew...

All of the Stone Crew got picked last year.

Mikey, the captain, in midfield.

They're going for it this year too.

Coach is gonna pick them again — for sure.

"Why we have to do this bullshit trial,
Mikey?" Sol asks.

"We just gonna get picked again."

"Yeah," says Momo. "Everyone knows it."

Mikey flicks up the ball. Holds it on his chest.

"People need reminding we're the best," he says.

Mikey lets the ball drop. Back heels it to Sol.

Then he looks at me.

"Plus we show the United fans round here how crap they are."

My team's United.

The Stone Crew laugh. They support City.

The whistle goes.

The players on the field jog off.

"Group C – you're on guys!" Mr Sands calls.

My turn now.

Chapter 2

Out on the pitch.

Mr Sands blasts his whistle again.

I begin to track the ball.

Win it clean – and run down the wing.

I'm feeling good.

A defender comes up.

I beat him with a drag back.

Beat another with a step over.

Try to cross – but another defender blocks it.

He kicks it away.

Then the ball is hit long to me.

I drift past the last defender — just on-side.

My first touch is good.

Second is better.

Only the keeper to beat...

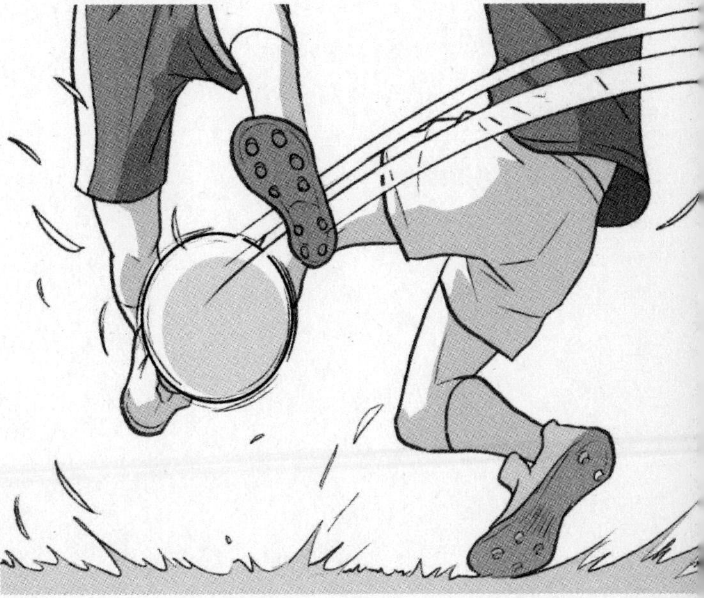

The keeper comes off his line.

I try to chip him.

The ball flies up —

— and over the bar.

"Yo! Amir! You chief!" Mikey shouts.

"That was an open goal!"

I'm gutted.

How did I miss?

The Stone Crew jeer as I track back.

But I keep on playing.

The whistle goes soon after.

Mr Sands calls us all over.

"OK guys, listen up," he says.

"In this year's Under 16's team..."

He calls out all of the Stone Crew.

No surprise there.

They all touch fists.

Then he calls out other names.

"...Robbie, Nihal, Cameron and Amir."

I follow the others to the locker room.

In shock.

In the team!

I can't stop smiling.

"What ya grinning at?" Mikey snaps at me.

"Guess I ain't so bad then…" I say.

Mikey pushes past me.

"Ya gonna get used to the subs bench!" he says.

But I'm still smiling.

I'm gonna prove him wrong.

Chapter 3

First game of the season.

We're beating the Bulls 2–0.

Ten minutes to go.

Mikey has scored. And Sol.

Mr Sands turns to me.

"Warm up Amir," he says. "You're going on."

It's what I've been waiting for.

I stretch and stamp.

Check my studs and shinpads.

The Hawks shirt feels good on my back.

The ball goes out of play.

"Sub, Ref?" Mr Sands calls. "Amir on — Momo off."

He waves to Momo.

Momo jogs slowly off the pitch.

"Great! Now we're playing with ten men!" Mikey says.

I go to slap Momo's hand as we pass.

But he blanks me.

Mikey holds his head.

I feel bad — but only for a moment.

I'm in the game.

Mikey wins the ball in midfield.

I lose my marker and make some space.

"Mikey!" I shout.

He keeps the ball, so I check my run.

"Mikey! I'm clear!" I yell.

But Mikey passes it to Sol.

He'd rather go back than pass to me?

"Sol!" I shout.

But Sol kicks it back to the keeper.

Back in the changing room, Mr Sands fronts Mikey.

"Why didn't you pass to Amir?" he asks.

Mikey shrugs, cool as you like.

"Didn't hear him call, Coach."

I give Mikey a look.

But he stares me out.

The others join in.

"None of us heard him call," says Jermaine.

"He's way too quiet," says Momo.

Mr Sands looks at me.

"Better call louder next time, Amir," he says.

And then he goes out.

I just wanna get outta there.

So I grab my gear.

Head for the door.

But Mikey is in my face.

"You ain't one of us — ya got no place in this team!" he says.

"Yeah — I ain't ever gonna pass to ya," calls Momo.

"Not even for a feel of Beyonce's booty!"

They all laugh so loud, everyone turns to stare.

"First one to pass to Amir has to lick my batty!"
Mikey goes on.

I don't wanna hear any more.

Slam the door behind me.

Chapter 4

I make my way to Tae Kwon Do.

Pass a poster for this Saturday's match.

United vs City — the local mash-up.

The poster's been tagged.

By Mikey and his crew.

No way I'm gonna leave that tag.

So I get out a marker.

Get even.

I get to Tae Kwon Do early.

Get changed into my gi.

I pair up with Caleb and bust my kicks.

No team.

Just me and my moves.

"Whoa — ya fired up!" Caleb says.

I nod.

Kick again.

Mikey and his crew fill my head.

What they did. What they said.

All those times they didn't pass to me...

I kick hard.

Miss the bag — my foot smashes into Caleb.

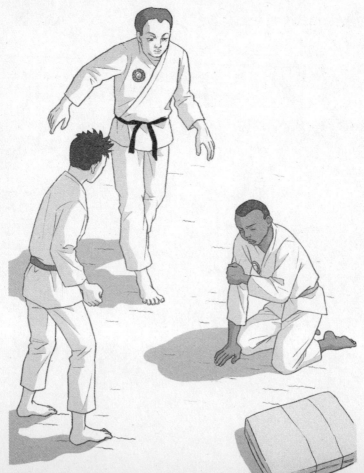

He ends up on the floor.

Gasping. In pain.

"Sorry, man," I say, shocked.

I try to help him up.

But he pushes me away.

"Ya need to chill, guy!" he snaps.

Mr Tang takes me to one side.

"Do you see the bag when you kick, Amir?" he asks.

"Or something else?"

Mr Tang is safe.

Gets respect from everybody.

I tell him about football.

About Mikey and his crew.

"I just wanna kick Mikey's butt!" I say.

"You have been sent a test, Amir," Mr Tang says.

"You must focus."

"Focus on what?" I ask him.

Mr Tang just smiles. "On what you know is right."

Chapter 5

Saturday comes and we're at the match.

Me and my cousins Kamil and Safia.

We run into Mikey and his crew.

One of the girls is Mikey's sister, Letisha.

She's in Safia's class.

"Yo, Safia!" Letisha calls.

Mikey glares at her.

Then he comes over to us.

"Ready for a beating?" he says.

"City is gonna carve United up — in its own backyard!"

I think of Mr Tang.

Don't rise to the bait.

I turn to Safia and Kamil.

"Let's find our seats," I say.

At half-time United are 2-0 up!

Best game for ages.

I spot Mikey and his crew.

Lined up for hotdogs.

None of them are smiling now.

Heads all low.

"Let's go over. Big it up!" says Kamil.

I grin. Then shake my head.

"No point looking for trouble," I say.

Then someone tugs my arm.

It's Safia — and she looks worried.

"Letisha and her friend, Jaki..." she says.

"I think they need help!"

I forget about Mikey and his crew.

"Show me," I say.

Chapter 6

Safia leads us out by the ladies toilet.

A bunch of drunk United fans are there.

Messing with Letisha and Jaki.

One of the guys makes a big show.

Looking them up and down.

"Ya ain't bad looking..." he says, "...for City fans."

His mates all snigger.

"Do ya feel as good as ya look?" says another guy.

He makes a grab at Letisha.

She slaps his hand away.

"Ya touch me, my brother gonna slap ya down!" she says.

But she sounds scared.

So I step in.

"Just quit it, guy," I say.

He lurches over to me.

"Who's gonna make me — you?" he sneers.

"If I have to," I say.

"Come on then!" the guy swipes out with his bottle.

I snap kick it out of his hand.

The bottle smashes on the ground.

The guy lunges forward.

My next kick lands in his belly.

Then he's on the floor.

Gasping for air.

His mates step up.

I'm ready.

"No — leave him," says the guy on the floor.

"Ain't gonna miss the game. Just coz some Paki thinks he's Jet Li."

He gets up.

"This ain't over, Paki," he snaps.

Then he turns to his mates. "Let's move it," he says.

He slopes off and the others follow.

Chapter 7

"Thanks..." Letisha says shakily.

Jaki nods. "Yeah, thanks..." she says.

"Want us to walk you back to the City stand?" I ask.

Letisha shakes her head. Gives me a little smile.

"No, we'll be OK. My brother's here now..."

I turn to see.

Mikey and his crew are standing there.

Watching.

With open mouths.

Letisha and Jaki walk over to them.

Some cleaner guy comes over.

He's got a pan and brush.

I help him sweep up the glass.

Then Mikey comes over.

"You looked out for my sister, man," he says.

He shakes his head.

As if he can't believe it.

"You chewed out a United fan — for *my* sister!"

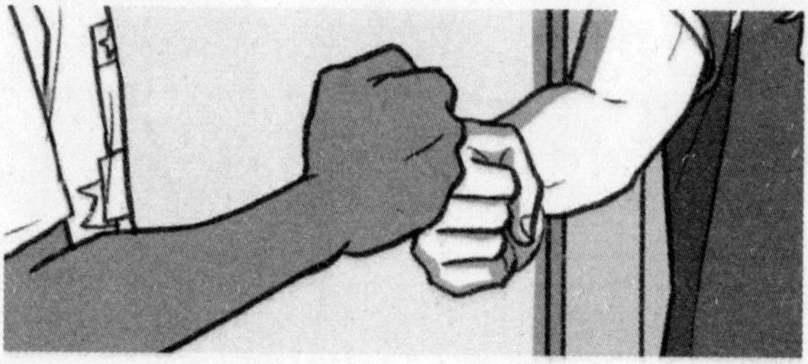

"Don't you get it, man?" I say.

I stand up. Look Mikey in the eye.

"That United fan — he was in the wrong.

Your sister — she needed help.

Nuff said."

"Come on Amir!" calls Kamil.

"Second half's starting!"

I turn away from Mikey.

We go our own ways.

The second half goes City's way.

Final score: 2–2.

"We were robbed!" says Kamil, as we leave.

"No, that penalty was fair," I tell him.

Kamil shakes his head.

"Dunno why you're sticking up for City!" he says.

I shrug.

Will the guy who dissed Letisha and Jaki
be outside?

The guy is there.

But Mikey has him in a headlock.

"And my sister told me what you said to Amir..."
Mikey's saying.

"Say it again and I'll fill ya mouth with my fist."

Sol puts a boot in.

Mikey turns and sees me. He grins.

Then lets the guy go — and takes off with
his crew.

Chapter 8

Monday comes round.

I walk to school — same as always.

Mikey and his crew are having a kickabout.

As I pass by, something hits me on the leg.

I sigh. What now?

I look down.

It's a football.

I turn back.

Mikey and his crew are all looking at me.

"What ya waiting for? Back to me!" Mikey shouts.

So I put my bag down.

Look at the ball.

Then I kick it.

Devon has two older brothers.

One rolls with the Endz Crew. The other is seeing a Viper Crew girl.

The two gangs don't mix.

Then someone pulls a gun...

978 0 7496 7712 1

More titles by Spike T. Adams:

978 0 7496 7713 8

978 0 7496 7714 5